FRANZESKA G. EWART

Bryony Bell
Tops the Bill

Bryony dreams of being a top-notch skater.
However she has to send back her new,
state-of-the-art skates to pay for her
sisters' costumes for *TV Family Star Turns*.
Poor Bryony. It's not much fun at school,
either. In the end of term play, she's cast
as the Ugly Ducking. Can the family's
fortunes – and Bryony's – turn in time
to give her the chance to strut her stuff?

First published 2004 by
A & C Black Publishers Ltd
37 Soho Square, London, W1D 3QZ

www.acblack.com

Text copyright © 2004 Franzeska G Ewart
Illustrations copyright © 2004 Kelly Waldek
The excerpt from *Big Spender* (Coleman/Fields) which appears
on page 39 is used with the kind permission of Campbell & Connelly.

ISBN 0-7136-6857-1

A CIP catalogue for this book is available from the British Library.

A&C Black uses paper produced with elemental chlorine-free
pulp, harvested from managed sustained forests.

Printed and bound in Spain by G. Z. Printek, Bilbao.

FRANZESKA G. EWART

Bryony Bell
Tops the Bill

Illustrated by Kelly Waldek

A & C Black • London

For Sharon Duncan, my oldest friend.

One

Bryony Bell thundered down the stairs three at a time. Four steps from the bottom she grabbed hold of the banister, flung herself over, took a running jump on to the mat in the middle of the polished wooden floor, and let it slide her smoothly to the front door. Then she clicked open the letterbox and hissed through at the rectangle of blue serge, 'Don't ring!'

The postman dutifully froze, and when Bryony opened the door he was still standing like a strange statue, index finger pointing bellwards.

'Shhhhh!' Bryony cautioned needlessly.

'Parcel for Ms B. Bell,' the postman whispered. 'You've to sign for it,' he added, almost inaudibly.

'Brilliant!' hissed Bryony. 'They've come!'

She signed the form.

'Don't want anyone knowing,' she explained as she handed it back. 'Top secret, it is – 'cept for my dad.'

The postman handed over a brown box covered in express delivery stickers, and hoisted his bag on to his shoulder. Then, with a muttered 'Mum's the word, then,' he shuffled off, leaving Bryony in her pink frilly nightie, gazing at the parcel in delight.

All was still quiet in the Bell household, but Bryony knew that time was running out. She made for the kitchen, ripped off the wrapping paper and read the writing on the box.

'Wicked!' she whistled. 'Viper 3000s with white fibreglass composite uppers, adjustable toe-stops, extra strong bearings and Ice-Lite wheels ...'

She opened the lid, lifted the white tissue paper, and gazed in wonder at what nestled within.

The early morning sun glinted off the shiny aluminium wheel-trims. The whole kitchen glowed in the dazzling whiteness of the fibreglass composite uppers. The wheels had 'speed' written all over their black rubber and the adjustable toe-stops looked strong enough to stop a herd of elephants in their tracks.

Bryony picked one up, held it to her nose and breathed in its delicious new smell. 'Viper 3000s ...' she whispered over and over to herself. 'White Viper 3000s – the ultimate in rollerskating perfection.'

She ripped back the Velcro strap, loosened the laces and slipped her foot inside. The rollerskate fitted like a glove. She took the other one out and put it on too, and, very slowly, she sidestepped gracefully round and round the table, first in one direction and then, backwards and considerably faster, in the other. She finished with a little spin, threw her head back, and, holding her nightie out with both hands, curtsied at the kettle, the fridge, and the bread-bin in turn.

'There's no stopping me now,' she said, smiling happily to herself. 'With Viper 3000s, the world's my oyster!'

She glanced upwards, head to one side, listening out for the familiar little creaking sound which meant her father was up. When she heard it, she blew a kiss in its direction and whispered, 'I love you, Dad!'

Hurrying now, she eased her feet out of the rollerskates and laid them gently back on their bed of tissue paper, just overcoming the temptation to kiss them too. Then she slid the box out of sight under the towels in the airing cupboard.

'Just in the nick of time!' she breathed, as a series of high-pitched sounds rent the air above her head.

She turned on the tap to fill the kettle. It was always best to do this during the 'voice exercises' because the gushing sound drowned out the worst of the top notes.

Then came 'scale practice'. During this, Bryony liked to be setting out the cereal bowls and jars of jam and marmalade and honey. And finally – and by this time she had to have the eggs on to boil and the bread in the toaster – there was the Bell Family Song.

The Bell Family Song rang out as usual, in close four-part harmony and with earsplitting gusto …

We're The Singing Bells and we'll sing till we drop
We're The Singing Bells and we're bound for the top
We're The Singing Bells and we'll try 'n try un-t-i-l
We get to the top...
We get to the top...
To the top of WHAT?

At this point there was the usual dramatic pause, during which Bryony tossed five teabags into the teapot then clamped her hands over her ears before the climax line:

WE GET TO THE...
T-O-P
O-F
T-H-E
B-I-L-L!!!!!!

'And after all that,' she muttered, pouring in the boiling water, 'they'll be absolutely ravenous.'

She set the teapot on the table, filled the milk jug and stood well back to watch the kitchen fill to the brim with little Bells.

There was Angelina Bell, who was nine, Melody and Melissa Bell, who were both eight, Emmy-Lou Bell, who was five, and 'Little' Bob Bell, who was two, and who came at the end, rather like a full stop. Following in the wake of his son and daughters was 'Big' Bob Bell, who was about the same height as Angelina and a full head shorter than Bryony.

'Right, now, take your cereal and mind your manners,' Big Bob shouted as he lifted Little Bob into his high chair. Soon the kitchen was filled with the sounds of *snaps*, *crackles* and *pops* of all descriptions. Big Bob sat down, looked over the sea of eaters, and caught Bryony's eye. He raised one eyebrow slightly, and Bryony raised one of hers in return. Then she lifted the milk jug and, coming round to his side of the table, bent over his shoulder to fill his bowl. And as she poured, she whispered conspiratorially, 'They've come, Dad! And they couldn't be better. Thanks a million trillion zillion!'

Big Bob grinned. 'That's my girl!' he whispered back. 'Oh Bryony,' he added, 'go easy on the butter on your mum's toast this morning. Bit of a heavy night at the Club, if you catch my drift.'

Bryony scraped some of the butter off the toast fingers she had prepared, carefully cut the top off one of the soft-boiled eggs, poured some very strong tea into a rose-patterned teacup, and set off upstairs with her mother's breakfast tray.

As she passed Big Bob he hissed, 'Just a minute, lass!' Then he grabbed a pair of scissors, rushed outside into the garden, and came back with a pink dewy rosebud and a huge proud smile.

'A rose for a rose,' he said, resting the stem against his little brown moustache and breathing in ecstatically, then popping the flower into a tiny vase and placing it reverentially on the tray between the soft-boiled eggs and the buttered toast fingers.

Bryony walked sedately upstairs. She eased the bedroom door open with her foot. The air inside was a musty mix of Air du Temps perfume and very old Newcastle Brown.

'Morning, Mum!' she said brightly.

Her mother groaned and heaved herself up on a multitude of pink silk pillows, each of which was embroidered with the letter C surrounded by garlands of pink rosebuds. She lifted one side of her black lace eyemask and said something that sounded like, '*Isthatthetime?*'

'Good audience?' Bryony asked tentatively.

'Not bad,' her mother replied. 'But it was such a late night, Bryony. I'm going to be shattered today, and we've a big rehearsal tonight for *TV Family Star Turns*. Did the little 'uns do their morning practice OK?'

Bryony nodded, and her mother smiled weakly.

'Only three weeks to go,' she said. 'Time's tight. Plump up my pillows will you Bryony? There's a love.'

Bryony laid her mother's tray on the floor, gritted her teeth, and began to thump.

'We'll do it though,' Clarissa went on, 'supposing it kills us. "That's show business", as they say!'

Bryony paused mid-punch, opened her mouth to speak, then closed it again. In dealings with Clarissa, timing, she knew, was everything – and this just wasn't the moment. Giving the pillow one final, colossal, thump she picked up the breakfast tray, set it on her mother's ample lap, and perched on the edge of the bed to wait till the time was ripe.

Nervously, she watched her mother eat the first boiled egg. A dozen or more photographs of her mother smiled back at her, for the bedroom was a veritable shrine to Clarissa Bell.

Clarissa Bell was her mother's stage name, her real name being Tracy which was way too ordinary. Most nights, Clarissa could be seen singing in a variety of working men's clubs, where she was enormously popular. Just like all the other Bells, Bryony thought her mum was magic, and she always loved to see her all dolled up. And Clarissa liked nothing better than to slip into a long slinky dress, coil up her wavy blonde hair high on her head like a luxurious cream dessert, and sing for them all. It made them all feel terribly special. And it made all of them – except Bryony – long for the day when they too would share in her fame.

All the Bell girls, except Bryony, had beautiful singing voices, and even Little Bob could gurgle his favourite song, *Bob the Builder*, well enough to be recognisable. Usually, it didn't bother Bryony – after all, she was going to be a skating star, nothing surer. But for the past month the Bell household had revolved around *The Singing Bells*. As far as Clarissa was concerned, thought Bryony ruefully, nothing else really mattered.

The Singing Bells was Clarissa's brainchild. She longed to see the family name up in lights, and when she had seen the advert for *TV Family Star Turns*, nothing would do but she would enter them. They had passed the first rounds with flying colours; and now that the live television final was just weeks away, they spent every spare minute practising.

It wasn't so bad, Bryony thought, being the only non-singing Bell girl – not when you had a brilliant dad who bought you mega-brilliant rollerskates. But, it was simply out of the question to ask that brilliant dad to buy you anything else...

TWO

Bryony took a deep breath. Time to take the bull by the horns.

'You know the play I'm in at school, Mum?' she said, leaning over to wipe a stray yolk dribble from Clarissa's chins.

'The one you're playing the lead in?' Clarissa said promptly. 'Like the family motto says,' she beamed at Bryony, "always a Bell at the top of the bill". You mark my words, Bryony – you'll shine at something, even if it isn't singing.'

Bryony wrinkled her nose. The play was another sore point. 'Anyway, Mum,' she said, not wanting to dwell on it, 'we're getting a disco after the last performance; it's going to be s-o-o-o-o-o cool. So ...' She gritted her teeth.

Her mother read her mind.

'You after a new dress, Bryony, love?'

Bryony nodded, but her mother shook her head sadly. 'Sorry, Bryony – absolutely out of the question. Your dad and I are going to have to spend every last penny in the Special Expenses Account on costumes for the little 'uns for *TV Family Star Turns*.

'It's the most important performance ever, Bryony,' she said, eyes glowing. 'The whole nation's going to see *The Singing Bells* for the very first time. And if we get the most votes, there's a recording contract and £50 000 in it. Just think of that!'

Bryony felt a guilty little shockwave zing up her back. She had never thought about *The Singing Bells* needing new outfits. And neither, evidently, had Dad. She felt her face glow red, right to the roots of her hair.

'But everybody's going to have new clothes 'cept me ...' she began, then her voice faded away hopelessly. How could she even have thought of asking?

Clarissa was not listening. She gazed into the distance, hands outstretched, oblivious to the crumbs and drips of yolk she was shedding on to the duvet cover.

'Just imagine it Bryony,' she murmured in a dreamy whisper, 'Angelina and Melody and Melissa, and Emmy-Lou and me, all singing on the telly together, and then the public phoning in and voting. Makes me wobbly to think of it! We've got to look just right.

'I fancy pink and sparkly myself,' she said decisively, 'but that kind of thing doesn't come cheap as you well know, and money – as ever – is as tight as a badger's bottom.'

She clinked the teacup onto the saucer with a note of finality.

'You'll just have to wear the blue one with the sailor's collar. Matches your eyes and sets off your hair.'

'But Mum,' Bryony wailed despite herself, 'the blue one's been handed down to Angelina!'

Clarissa wiped her mouth on the lace-trimmed napkin and replaced the eye mask. 'Well, it'll just have to be handed back up again,' she said grimly, pulling the duvet up round her chin to indicate that breakfast, and the audience, was well and truly over.

Bryony gathered up the tray and plodded back downstairs with a heavy heart. Of course she couldn't have a new dress. Of course it was far more important that *The Singing Bells* looked just right.

Of course it was. But still, it was a crying shame.

* * *

'Want a lift to school, Bryony, love?' Big Bob asked as she reached the hall.

Bryony shook her head. 'Not today, thanks, Dad – I'll go on my old rollerskates.' She took hold of Big Bob's arm and steered him away from the front door, where the rest of the family had assembled ready to be transported to their various destinations.

'Dad?' she whispered worriedly, 'can we really afford the Vipers?'

Big Bob laughed and ruffled her hair. "Course we can!' he said. 'What else have I got to spend money on than my special princess?'

Bryony swallowed. 'Costumes for *TV Family Star Turns*?' she said quietly, looking at her feet.

Big Bob's jaw dropped.

'Oh my goodness, Bryony!' he gasped. 'It never crossed my mind.'

'They have to have costumes, Dad,' Bryony said. 'And Mum says money is as tight as a badger's bottom.'

Big Bob's bald patch blushed bright crimson. 'Well now,' he said, giving a little cough, 'I wouldn't put it quite like that but ... ' He sighed and put a hand on Bryony's shoulder as though she might be about to fall. 'Perhaps under the circumstances, Bryony, love, we'll have to return the Vipers for the time being.'

Then, looking utterly crestfallen, he turned towards the door, shooed the little Bells into the van and swept Little Bob up and under his arm. Bryony clung on to his belt and followed him, the full horror of what was about to happen suddenly hitting home.

'But Dad ...' she said, close to tears. 'I haven't even tried them. I've only skated twice round the kitchen table!'

'It's a sin, I know,' her father said, sliding the van door closed, 'but it just can't be helped. We'll discuss it tonight.'

'It says on the box you can return them after fourteen days if you're not entirely satisfied!' Bryony whispered desperately. 'Can I not keep them for a bit? I'll not get them scuffed – I'll just use them in my bedroom... please Dad!'

'All right, Bryony,' Big Bob hissed back at her with a wink, 'they're yours for a fortnight. But don't breathe a word to the others, mind!'

'Thanks Dad,' breathed Bryony gratefully. 'I won't tell a living soul.'

Big Bob opened the driver's door and hauled himself up and in. When he had closed the door he rolled down the window and poked his head out.

'And mark my words Bryony – one day they'll be yours for keeps,' he whispered under his breath, 'or my name's not Bob Bell!'

Then, with a cough and a roar and a spray of gravel, he drove away.

* * *

Bryony fetched the Viper 3000s from the airing cupboard and took them upstairs, where she hid them under her bed. Sitting in front of her dressing table mirror, she brushed her long blonde curls vigorously and gathered them into two very pert bunches, each secured with a silky pink and white orchid. She smiled bravely at her reflection; and her reflection smiled bravely back at her, and winked.

It could be worse, she thought to herself. Some people never got to wear Viper 3000s – and she had them for a whole fortnight. And some people didn't even have a handed-back sailor dress to wear to a disco after their school play.

At the thought of the school play Bryony shook her head, got up, and strapped on her everyday black rollerskates. She wasn't even going to think about the school play. That could really push her over the edge.

Humming tunelessly to keep her spirits up she set off for school, skating sedately along until she reached the end of the road. When she had turned the corner and was out of sight of prying neighbours' eyes, she picked up speed. Checking that the pavement was relatively empty, she balanced on the outside edges of her right foot, stretched her left leg straight out behind her, and glided towards the kerb where she jumped, spun in mid-air, and landed with her back to the road. Then, pushing off on her left foot and with her right leg in the air, she executed an elegant curve round the postman, finishing with a forward arabesque.

The postman stopped and watched her in admiration.

'That's pure genius, Bryony Bell,' he said, putting his bag down in wonder. 'Poetry in motion, that is. Going to let me see a spin, then?'

'Sure,' said Bryony. 'Hang on!' She handed him her schoolbag and skated backwards. Then she stopped, struck a pose with one arm in the air and the other across her waist, and pushed off hard. When she was within a metre of the postman's feet she stretched her arms out wide, moved her right foot in front of her left, snapped her arms against her sides, and spun so fast her hair looked like a big blonde blur.

When Bryony finally unwound herself, the postman applauded loudly.

'You're going to be a star, Bryony Bell, and no mistake,' he told her admiringly, handing her back the schoolbag as though it was a gold cup.

'Thanks,' said Bryony, giving a little bow. 'I intend to be.'

And she glided down the street, negotiated her way between the schoolchildren milling around outside the school gates, and made her entrance – backwards – into the playground of Peachtree Primary.

Three

For the rest of the week all Bryony thought about was getting home from school to try the Viper 3000s.

Her bedroom carpet was not the best surface for skating, but even on shagpile the Vipers were wonderful. Taking care not to scuff the boots, she worked out a routine in front of the wardrobe mirror and, with one eye on her reflection, practised it to perfection. And every time she took the Vipers off and laid them back in their box, she felt a sharp pang of regret as she thought how little time she had left with them.

On Friday morning she set off sadly for school and, as she always did, scanned the playground for the towering figure of Abid Ashraf. Abid, who was Bryony's closest friend, was possibly the largest boy of his age anywhere in the universe. He was also one of the most solemn. This morning he looked more than usually miserable.

'What's wrong, Abid?' Bryony asked. 'You do look peaky.'

Abid looked down at Bryony, his brown eyes deeply melancholic. 'Don't look so perky yourself, Bryony. Anything wrong?'

Bryony shook her head and grinned. 'Oh, I'm OK,' she told Abid. 'You know me – nothing gets me down for long!'

The line moved towards the door and Abid followed it, trailing his big feet. Bryony skated behind him, pushing, as she did every morning.

Secretly Bryony was sure that, without her steady pressure, Abid would never ever make it to the boys' cloakroom.

'It's my asthma, Bryony,' he told her gloomily,

'and my excema. They're awful just now. I sneeze and itch and wheeze and sneeze and itch and wheeze – and nothing my father gives me does any good!'

'You'd think having a father who's a doctor would mean you were never ill, but it doesn't seem to work in your case,' Bryony observed. 'Come to think of it, mine's a joiner and all our doors squeak.'

'Well, of course you know what's causing it, don't you?' Abid said pointedly.

Bryony nodded. She knew all right. And when she thought about it, she felt another dark cloud descend to add to the ones that hung over the Viper 3000s and the blue sailor dress.

For what seemed like a lifetime, Bryony and Abid's class had been practising their end-of-term musical play, *The Ugly Duckling*. It was to be performed next week and today was the first full dress rehearsal, so as soon as the register had been called they all lined up with their costumes and were marched to the hall. Bryony trailed along at the back, the little dark clouds following her, and Abid trailed even more slowly behind her, looking as though he was going to have all his teeth extracted.

The stage had been transformed into a lakeside scene. There was a vivid blue backdrop with bright green trees and crimson flowers, and a very yellow sun. A blue cloth had been spread on the floor, with larger-than-life bulrushes growing round its edge and big pink waterlilies arranged on its surface. It all looked most effective.

They were given a few minutes to get into their costumes. In the past weeks Bryony had managed to keep an eye on Abid during this procedure, and had pinned his costume on as best she could, but today Mrs Ogilvie, the class teacher, insisted that boys change on one side of the stage and girls on the other. With a grim expression on her face, and a pincushion attached to her wrist, she had led Abid away into the darkness behind the curtains. Abid looked back, managing a brave smile and a 'thumbs up' sign. As the lights dimmed, the words 'lamb to the slaughter' popped into Bryony's head.

When Mrs Ogilvie announced that all was ready, Mrs Quigg the music teacher, played three loud notes on the piano and in the semi-darkness two yellow ducklings made their entrances and shuffled about, whispering nervously. Bryony gritted her teeth and pulled her mask over her head.

'Where is the Ugly Duckling?' Mrs Quigg shouted, playing the cue music again. 'Where is Bryony Bell?'

Slowly, Bryony waddled on. Like the two

yellow ducklings, she wore a big duck mask and orange tights. Unlike the yellow ducklings, she wore a costume made of grey-brown feathers.

'You have missed your cue again, Bryony,' Mrs Quigg told her angrily. 'Remember, you are the star of the show. Now, sing!'

Bryony flapped her grey-brown wings gloomily as the music began, and hung her head down so low that her chin was on her chest.

'That's right,' said Mrs Quigg happily. 'Look miserable.'

'Oh I'm an Ugly Duckling,' sang Bryony, in a gravelly monotone,
'And no one wants me near.
My drab and dowdy feathers
Make all the ducklings sneer!'

The yellow ducklings waddled round the lake, making spitting noises and pointing rudely at Bryony. At the edge of the pond was a log which had been made by covering two benches with painted corrugated paper and artificial flowers. On it sat a line of six children dressed as frogs in green lycra costumes, flippers, and wide-mouthed, large-eyed masks. At this point in the play they all had to nudge one another and laugh at Bryony, which they always did extremely enthusiastically – so much so that, more often than not, one of them fell off the log. Mrs Quigg had high hopes that as long as they didn't overdo it, this part of the show would bring the house down.

Suddenly something inside Bryony snapped. She pushed her mask to the back of her head, put her hands on her hips, marched to the front of the stage, and glared down at the music teacher.

'The Ugly Duckling isn't the star part, Mrs Quigg,' she said firmly. 'The swan is the star part. Please, Mrs Quigg, can't I please be the swan?' And under her breath she muttered, 'Ducks suck.'

Mrs Quigg sighed. 'Look, Bryony,' she said, 'I've told you a dozen times – Abid is the swan. Abid has a lovely big swan voice, Abid knows all the words of *The Swan Song* and sings it so sweetly it brings tears to the eyes, and Abid never, ever misses his cues.'

She sat down on the piano stool heavily. 'Furthermore,' she added wearily, 'Abid is the only person big enough for the swan costume. Now let that be an end to it.' And she played three ferocious chords, just to make the point.

Bryony stood her ground, wondering whether to fall to her knees and plead for the part, which was the only tactic she had not yet used. Everyone knew that Mrs Quigg, unlike Mrs Ogilvie, was open to wheedling, but so far all Bryony's attempts to wrest the swan part from Abid had failed. Finally, as Mrs Quigg continued to thump the piano keys ever more violently, Bryony admitted defeat.

She moved slowly back into her position centre stage and glanced over into the wings where, in the gloom, the huge, white, feathery shape of Abid stood waiting for his entrance. To her horror, she noticed that he had his legs tightly crossed.

'Cue *The Frogs' Chorus*!' Mrs Quigg yelled. 'And pick Jeremy up this instant!' She thumped the first bars and the six frogs began to croak in unison. Bryony edged closer to the side of the stage and hissed at Abid, 'What's the matter?'

Abid sneezed twice, wheezed painfully, and

muttered miserably, 'I need the toilet Bryony – and she's sewn me in!'

Bryony looked desperately around, but Mrs Ogilvie had temporarily vanished. Below the stage she could see Mrs Quigg's grey curls, bouncing gaily in time to the music. The frogs were well into their stride, bobbing up and down as they croaked.

'Mrs Quigg!' she called, flapping her stubby little brown wings.

Mrs Quigg, however, was soaring on the wings of song and remained oblivious.

'Mrs Quigg!' Bryony yelled again. 'Nature calls! The swan can not make his entrance!'

That was the last straw. With a hysterical roar the music teacher froze mid-chord. Then she slammed down the piano lid, and with a tearful toss of her head flounced out of the hall.

'YOU ARE SUPPOSED TO GO BEFORE YOU COME!' she shrieked as she made her exit. 'I can not work with all these interruptions. It's simply ruining my creative flow!'

And she disappeared, leaving the rehearsal in the stouter hands of Mrs Ogilvie who had appeared in the very nick of time.

Four

As soon as Mrs Quigg had gone, the atmosphere on stage eased as Mrs Ogilvie took charge.

'Take five!' she told them, brandishing the pinking shears in the direction of Abid's seams.

Five minutes later, Bryony and a much-relieved Abid were sitting together on the frogs' log, waiting to be told what to do next. Abid's abandoned downy-white costume lay at their feet.

'I can't bear being the swan,' Abid sighed, shaking his head in abject misery. 'I'm scared I'll forget the words of the song, and I'm scared I'll need the toilet, and I'm scared I'll start to sneeze. They can say what they like Bryony,' he went on miserably, 'I'm not cut out for show business. I want to be an accountant or a brain surgeon. I just hate people looking at me, you know?'

'Ironic, isn't it,' Bryony said, nodding sympathetically. 'I'd just love to be the swan, as you well know. Makes shivers run down my spine just thinking about making that entrance and singing *The Swan Song*. Except I can't sing.' She sighed deeply. 'You know, Abid – sometimes it seems to me that you don't get anywhere in this life if you can't sing.'

She gave the grey-brown feathers of her duck costume a swipe. 'And I just hate this costume,' she growled. 'Not one ounce of star quality!' Then she ran her fingers through the bright silvery-white swan feathers and gave a shiver of delight. 'It must be wonderful to wear your one – like being inside a wedding cake!'

Abid shuddered. 'It's not. It's awful! I can't breathe in the mask, and bits of feather keep wafting up and making me sneeze. That's what's going for my tubes, Bryony – I know it. That and nerves.'

'Then tell her,' said Bryony, giving Abid's orange knee a little thump with her wing. 'Tell her you can't be a swan on medical grounds. Tell her you're more suited to a frog part. I would.'

Abid shook his head in misery. 'I can't, Bryony. She's got her heart set on having a great big swan soprano, and I just can't let her down.'

He gazed down at his huge orange feet. 'It has to be faced, Bryony – there's no one who can step into my shoes.'

They sat in silence for a while, meditating on

the unfairness of life. Then, in an attempt to cheer Abid up, Bryony said brightly, 'What are you wearing for the party?'

It had the opposite effect. Abid's head sunk further on to his chest.

'A green salwar kameez with gold and silver trim,' he told her gloomily, adding by way of explanation. 'Mum's made it.'

'Oh,' Bryony said. She couldn't think of anything better than having a mother who sewed beautiful silky clothes with glittery trimmings. 'Sounds cool to me. Better than last season's sailor dress that smelly Angelina's worn, anyway!'

Abid considered this for a moment. 'Just between ourselves, Bryony,' he said confidentially, 'I think it's a bit ostentatious. I'd rather wear a plain grey one, or jeans and a t-shirt. But you know how it is – you can't hurt their feelings, can you?'

Bryony nodded. For a while they sat in silence, watching Jeremy peel off his green lycra. Jeremy was a rather small child and his 'one-size-fits-all' costume did not cling like the other frogs' did, but hung in wrinkles round his waist and knees. The costumes fastened down the back with velcro and each frog was supposed to help another out and in, but Jeremy had been abandoned and was lying on his back with his legs in the air, rocking helplessly. Bryony wandered over and ripped him free.

'You wouldn't get me in jeans for any money,' she said as she rejoined Abid. 'I'm just a sucker for silk. Bright pink silk—' she went on dreamily, '—all wafty and floaty, with lace and bows and sequins ...'

Mrs Quigg, blotchy-faced and swollen-eyed, had returned and was dabbing her nose with a lacy handkerchief and banging the lid of the piano up and down.

'Places, please, for Scene Three!' she shouted, and everyone sighed and moved into position again. Neither Abid nor Bryony were on stage till the very end, so they prepared to shuffle off.

'Guess what, Abid,' Bryony whispered as she helped Abid scoop up his feathers. 'I'm not really supposed to tell a living soul, but that doesn't include you, of course: I've got new rollerskates. White ones. Viper 3000s – the best rollerskates in the world!'

Abid tried to look cheerful.

'Oh, that's wonderful, Bryony,' he said. 'Will they make you skate even better?'

'Not half,' said Bryony, holding the curtain aside to let Abid into the wings. 'They've got extra ball-bearings for really smooth wheel action, and fibreglass composite uppers, combining lightness with strength. Imagine - they even go on shagpile!'

'They're wonderful,' she said, then sighed. 'But they've got to go back in a week. Every penny has to go to getting *The Singing Bells* their glitzy costumes for the telly. I'm trying to look on the bright side, but it's not easy.'

To Abid's surprise Bryony took off her duck mask, threw back her head, and balanced on one leg. She stretched the other one out behind her as high as she could, clasping both hands to her chest.

'Doesn't this look elegant, Abid?' she shouted over the noise of the Farmyard Chorus on stage. 'And just imagine how much more elegant it looks with sparkling-white roller boots ...'

Abid opened his mouth to assure Bryony that it looked extremely elegant, and sneezed instead. But Bryony wasn't listening. She had had the most incredible flash of inspiration.

'There's no-one can step into my shoes,' Abid had said. All of a sudden, Bryony wasn't so sure. She peeked through the curtain to make sure she wasn't missing her next cue, then moved closer to Abid.

'Know what, Abid,' she whispered mysteriously, tapping the side of her nose. 'I think your troubles may be over.

'I have hit on the most breathtakingly-brilliant, scintillating-surefire gem of an idea ...'

Five

All the way home Bryony thought about the idea. Abid had smiled as enthusiastically as he ever did when he heard it, and had said politely that it really was a breathtakingly-brilliant, scintillatingly-surefire gem of an idea and that he would be eternally grateful to her. She was, he had added, the very best and cleverest friend anyone could ever have.

She skated slowly, pausing every so often to do a thoughtful little pirouette. Abid's gratitude put a lot of pressure on her to make the gem-of-an-idea work, and now, in the clear light of day, she realised it was not going to be all that easy. There was very little time left, and a great deal of work to do. And it was fraught with risks and complications – but then, she told herself as she neared the house, weren't all breathtakingly-brilliant, scintillatingly-surefire plans?

Today's practice was already under way, and through the open window drifted the strains of the song that Angelina, Melody, Melissa and Emmy-Lou did on their own. It was called *Devoted Sisters*.

At the end of that song, Angelina would announce, 'And now, ladies and gentlemen, the moment you've all been waiting for. Please welcome … '

And each sister in turn would wheel round to face stage left, go down on one knee, and sing a syllable – each syllable higher than the one before so they formed a chord:

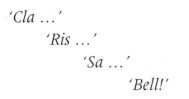

> *'Cla …'*
>   *'Ris …'*
>   *'Sa …'*
>   *'Bell!'*

As they held the notes, Clarissa would make her entrance, swaying luxuriously from side to side, and in a voice husky with emotion and deep with mystery, would sing …

'The minute you walked in the joint...'

and the little 'uns would chorus, *'Boom! Boom!'* Then Clarissa would heave her hips to right and left, and when the last line rang out,

'Hey! Big Spender... s-p-e-n-d a little time with me!'
they would all join in and swing their little hips

in time with hers.

When they sang the *Devoted Sisters* song, the little 'uns did a special dance, which Bryony had helped to choreograph and which involved a lot of arm-linking and leg-kicking, and they tried very hard to sway exactly in time with the music. It had been coming along very nicely, and every time they finished Big Bob had to take out his handkerchief and say, 'Bring a tear to a glass eye, that would', and dab his, just to prove it.

Bryony smiled as she made out the first words:

Who's always there when you're feeling blue?
When life gets tough, who sees you through?
Who is the one who's d-e-v-o-t-e-d to you?
Your sister – that's who!

Melody and Melissa were about to go into the chorus, which listed the many ways they had of showing their sisterly devotion, when Bryony opened the front door. As soon as it clicked shut the singing stopped, and the twins thundered through into the hall, followed by the other two devoted sisters. When they saw Bryony they all stopped and glared malevolently at her.

Bryony stopped in her tracks. What now?

Angelina stepped forward, her hands on her hips. 'We can't get nice glitzy stage costumes for

TV Family Star Turns and it's all because of you!' she shrieked. She was shaking with anger, and the beads on her long braids flew about and clinked together, making her look like a snake-headed gorgon.

'It's just not fair!' screamed Melody, linking arms with Melissa.

'And another thing – Melody and me need hair extensions,' Melissa added, in a particularly whiney voice. 'Now that's down the tube too!'

'You have snatched fame from beneath our feet, Bryony Bell,' Angelina said grimly, slipping her arm round Melody's waist. Emmy-Lou, two fat tears poised to pop out of her huge blue eyes, clung to the straps of Angelina's octopus jeans.

Then they all clung silently together like a small, furious, chorus-line, almost spitting venom at Bryony.

'Hang on, hang on,' Bryony said, putting her hand on Emmy-Lou's curly little head. 'Let's not jump to conclusions.'

'Mum told us,' Melissa whined. Melissa had a very long fringe which always hung in front of her eyes. When she put on her whiny face – which she quite often did – Big Bob said she looked like a Cairn terrier with distemper.

'She said she found out when she went to the bank to withdraw money from the Special Expenses Account and there was ...' Melissa inhaled deeply and wetly, but before she had sucked in enough air to go on Emmy-Lou concluded, in a voice choked with tears,

'... not a sodding brass farthing!'

'That's what Mum said,' Melody put in. 'So don't dare deny it!'

'It's downright criminal,' Angelina went on. 'Here we all are, bursting with talent, destined to become the stars of the future; and now that destiny is hanging in the balance –and why?' She pressed her forefinger against Bryony's chest and prodded her hard in time with each syllable: 'Your sel-fish-ness, Bry-o-ny Bell!'

'Mum says you can twist Dad round your little finger,' Melissa whined.

'So?' said Bryony, removing Angelina's finger and trying to push past them all. 'Why shouldn't I get new skates? My old ones are nipping my toes and the ball-bearings have gone and the wheel stops sometimes don't. Just because you're going to be big TV stars. Just because I can't sing...'

Bryony stopped as Clarissa swept downstairs with Little Bob in her arms. Immediately, everyone except Emmy-Lou straightened up and tried to look innocent.

'Sure Bryony's to give the skates back this very minute, Mum?' Emmy-Lou said, reaching up to clasp Clarissa's hand. 'Sure she is?'

Bryony gasped in utter horror. They couldn't. They simply couldn't.

A terrible silence descended. Even Little Bob stopped gurgling and pointed a chubby, wet and accusing little finger at her. Bryony appealed to Clarissa.

'Dad said I could keep them for another week. Oh Mum, please ...'

But Clarissa shook her head, clamped her lips tightly together, and sucked all the air out of her cheeks. Bryony's heart plummeted. This did not auger at all well.

'I'm sorry, Bryony,' Clarissa said at last, her voice shaky. 'It's a question of priorities. If we win *TV Family Star Turns*, the first thing we'll do is buy you the Viper 3000s again. But we have to have costumes, Bryony. We need to match, and we need to look glamorous. You know what the telly's like – it's all image.' She sighed. 'It's a real shame, love, I know.'

'But Mum,' Bryony tried again, 'I need the Vipers. I've got an idea and without the Vipers it just won't work. Just one more week ... '

Clarissa was not to be moved.

'I know you, Bryony. You'll say you won't scuff them, but you will. Fetch them,' she said, kindly but firmly. 'With the box. Your father will take them to the post office first thing tomorrow morning.'

Then she turned to the other children, her eyebrows high and her emerald green eye-shadow flashing a warning. 'And if I hear one more word about this from you lot, I'm warning you – there'll be hell to pay. This is not easy for Bryony. Understood?'

Angelina and Melody blushed deeply and looked at their toes contritely. Melissa opened her mouth to whine and had her foot stepped on by Melody. Emmy-Lou nodded sagely and said, 'We hear you, Mum.' Then they all muttered their apologies and trailed back into the living room to rekindle the flames of sisterly devotion.

Eyes burning, Bryony climbed the stairs. Never had the clouds above her head seemed so dark. When she got to her bedroom she knelt down and slid out the Viper 3000s box, lifted the lid for the last time and watched her tears fall at last, to lie sparkling like diamonds on the white fibreglass composite uppers.

'Sorry, Abid,' she whispered as she laid the rollerskates to rest, covered them over with tissue paper, and said goodbye.

When she plodded back down to hand them over, Clarissa took the box with a reassuring smile. 'Chin up, Bryony,' she said. 'We're bound to win, and then you'll get them back.'

'Is Dad home yet?' Bryony asked.

'I believe he is,' said Clarissa frostily. 'I'd check the potting shed, if I were you. And tell him his dinner's on, though I'm blowed if he deserves it.'

Six

'Oh Dad...'

Big Bob was sitting in the shed on a tea-chest padded with faded gold cushions, polishing his big brown boots. When he saw her, he gave Bryony such a sympathetic look that she nearly burst into tears all over again. Putting the shoe brush back in the box by his side, he wiped his dungarees and patted his knee. Bryony perched precariously on it, leaning on his shiny little bald patch to balance herself.

'Talk about being in the doghouse, Bryony,' Big Bob sighed. 'Didn't expect your mum to go looking at the Special Expenses Account this week.'

'Do I really twist you round my little finger, Dad?' Bryony asked suddenly, hooking her pinkie under Big Bob's shirt collar and tugging. 'Did I really wheedle at you till you got me the Vipers?'

Big Bob patted Bryony's back and smiled.

'Not a bit of it, lass,' he assured her. Then he

lowered his voice. 'Just between you and me and the potting compost,' he whispered, 'I sometimes think *The Singing Bells* go a bit over the score, so to speak.

'The little 'uns are really mad at me, Dad,' Bryony said. 'It's like they think I'm a traitor.' She gave a long sigh. 'Well, maybe I am. Maybe we both are – not thinking they'd need costumes.'

'There's more to life than being able to sing, Bryony,' Big Bob said comfortingly. 'When God was giving out vocal chords, you and me weren't too far up the queue. So, singing's just not in our genes and that's all there is to it. But that doesn't mean you can't be a star – you mark my words!'

'I think you're a star,' Bryony said, smiling bravely. 'But Dad,' she went on, 'there's another problem. The Vipers are vital for the success of a plan I've got, and now Mum says they've got to go back tomorrow.'

'A plan, Bryony, love?'

Bryony slipped off Big Bob's knee, shifted the box of shoe-cleaning materials, and knelt at his feet.

'It's my pal Abid Ashraf. You know - the big shy quiet one? Got asthma and a lovely singing voice and doesn't like being looked at?'

Big Bob nodded. ''Course I know Abid,' he

said. 'Heart of gold, that boy, and clever with it. So what's up, Bryony?'

'He's got to play the swan part in the school play and it's making him really miserable, and I had this idea that I could do it - on skates! You know – really smooth 'n' elegant, balancing on one leg a lot and with loads of arabesques. And Abid could still sing, but he'd be offstage so no one could see, so he wouldn't feel embarrassed.

'If only Mrs Quigg had seen the Viper 3000s,' she sighed. 'That would have clinched it. The swan costume's white, you see.'

'Sure, Bryony,' said Big Bob thoughtfully. 'I get the picture.'

He put his hands on his knees and rocked to and fro, whistling through the gap in his front teeth. He always did that when he was thinking, and Bryony sat silently, hopefully, waiting. Sure enough, after a few moments the whistling stopped and Big Bob leapt to his feet, gave his thigh a swipe, and said 'Yeeee-hah!' – which was what he always did when inspiration struck.

'Actions speak louder than words – that's the key to it!' he beamed. 'Like when I was courting your mother. Flipping terrified, I was, to ask her to marry me – she being a singer, you know, and me just a humble joiner. So, guess what I did?'

'What?' said Bryony, eyes sparkling.

Big Bob glanced at the shed door and lowered

his voice. 'Went out and spent half my wage packet on a bouquet of red roses, then got down on one knee and presented her with them!'

And he lowered himself down on his right knee to demonstrate.

'So a bunch of flowers did it?' Bryony asked. 'As easy as that?'

'Well ... not just a bunch of flowers,' Big Bob told her with a wink. 'Right in the middle of the roses, I hid a box. And when your mum opened it, what do you think there was inside but a ruby ring, winking up at her from the black velvet lining. Like a tiny beating heartful of love, that ruby was. Cleaned me out for years Bryony, but it did the trick!'

Bryony gazed dreamily at her father. 'That is so romantic, Dad. But what's it got to do with me and old Mrs Quigg? Sure as anything I'm not marrying her!'

'What I said, Bryony: actions speak louder than words. You have to do the dance for her, never mind telling her about it. Catch her off her guard then dazzle her – bowl her over – like I did with your mother! OK?'

'Without the Viper 3000s, though?'

Big Bob rummaged about among the shoe-cleaning materials and took out a tube.

'Fetch your old skates, lass,' he told her. 'Your dad'll fix it!'

* * *

After four coats of shoe whitener, the black skates looked marginally better. Big Bob held them up hopefully.

'Well...' said Bryony, 'I suppose they'll have to do. Oh – by the way, Dad – dinner must be ready. We'd better not be late.'

Big Bob set the skates on top of some plant pots to dry and heaved himself up. But just as Bryony opened the shed door he motioned to her to come back to the tea-chest. Suddenly very serious, he sat down and took both her hands in his.

'Before we go in, I want a word with you, Bryony lass,' he said. 'A serious word.'

He cleared his throat a number of times and Bryony frowned down at him.

'What is it, Dad?' she said. 'What's wrong?'

In answer, Big Bob asked her a question. 'All this *Singing Bells* telly stuff, Bryony – is it bothering you? You feeling a bit left out?'

Bryony hesitated. It was on the tip of her tongue to smile and say, 'Not a bit of it, Dad – water off a duck's back!' as she would usually have done. But today the words stuck in her throat.

'I don't care about not being in *The Singing Bells*,' she whispered, as much to herself as to Big Bob. 'I don't care about not being on the telly and not getting a glitzy costume and not taking a big bow with Mum and the little 'uns.' Her voice faltered. All the little dark clouds seemed to have merged into one huge one, which had squeezed itself into the potting shed to hang heavily above her head.

Big Bob gave her arms a gentle squeeze.

'Because you know, lass,' he went on huskily, as though Bryony had not spoken at all, 'that if you did mind, it would be quite OK. No harm in thinking about yourself now and then, Bryony ... Mmmm?'

Bryony nodded, then gave a very loud, long sniff. In the distance, a gong called out to them across the garden, drowning out the birds' evening songs then fading to an eerie echo. When Bryony looked back at Big Bob, she noticed with surprise how very blue his eyes were. Blue, like hers, she thought for the first time.

Filled with tears like hers, too.

'I do, Dad,' Bryony admitted at last. 'I mind.'

Big Bob nodded. 'That's my girl,' he said. 'Better out than in.'

The gong's echo vanished and was replaced by a chorus of high-pitched voices trilling 'It's time for tea!' tunefully. Big Bob got up, and they both moved slowly towards the door and out.

'Remember what I said about actions speaking louder than words, Bryony?' Big Bob said, as he closed the shed door behind them. 'Tomorrow morning, know what I reckon you should do?'

'What, Dad?'

As they made their way along the path, Big Bob rested his stubbly chin on Bryony's shoulder and whispered in her ear. And, later, as she squeezed a fat worm of tomato ketchup onto her fish and chips, Bryony looked round the table and remembered everything he had said.

She smiled to herself as she munched her battered cod. Tomorrow morning was going to be different from all other mornings, she thought. Tomorrow morning, Bryony just knew, that big dark cloud was going to get itself a silver lining.

Seven

The next day was Saturday, and on Saturdays singing practice began an hour later than on weekdays because *The Singing Bells* needed their beauty sleep.

Bryony was up at the crack of dawn as usual, however. She had work to do. The night before, she had carefully extracted the middle pages from her Maths homework book, and pencilled in some ideas. Before breakfast these ideas had been revised, redrafted, and neatly rewritten in a variety of colours of felt tip pen.

That done, she held the completed sheet up and checked to see that it all worked properly. It did – like a dream. Bryony smiled with satisfaction. She had created a perfectly failsafe system, and the hour was fast approaching when she would put that system into action. Breaking off a small piece of Blu-Tak from the slab on her desk she set off downstairs with a spring in her step. Things were about to change in the Bell household, she thought grimly. It wasn't going to be popular, but there was going to be a bit of equality at last. And a bit more time to call her own.

No sooner had she arrived in the kitchen than *The Singing Bells* began their practice. Bryony beamed as she watched the water gush into the kettle. She hummed to herself as she set out the cereal bowls, running a spoon along their sides in time with the voice exercises. Deftly, she caught the slices of toast as they shot into the air and juggled with them on their way to Clarissa's tray. And when the strains of the Bell Family Song rang out she joined in lustily, throwing an extra teabag into the pot, just to celebrate.

'Morning, Bryony! How's my princess?'

Big Bob was first down for a change, the Viper 3000s box under his arm, and when he saw Bryony he gave her a 'Well, then?' kind of look.

'Mission accomplished, Dad,' Bryony grinned back, nodding in the direction of the toaster. The piece of paper and the Blu-Tak were hidden behind it, ready for the Moment of Truth.

'Morning, Angelina,' Bryony brightly greeted the first sister to appear.

'Good morning, Bryony,' Angelina said with frosty politeness, one eye on Big Bob.

'I trust you slept well?' Bryony enquired. 'You certainly sound in excellent voice.'

Angelina darted a suspicious look in Bryony's direction, but Bryony smiled charmingly as she passed her the milk jug.

All the other little Bells took their seats, each glaring at Bryony and then exchanging glances with one another. You could have cut the atmosphere with a knife.

They all began to eat in stony silence. 'I think,' said Big Bob at last, putting his toast down wearily, 'we might let the matter of the Viper 3000s rest now? They're here in their box, and I'm posting them back to Sk8s 'R' Us this morning. Neither your sister nor I ever set out to rob you of your chances of fame and fortune, as I'm sure you know, and we deeply regret any anxiety our actions may have caused. 'So – water under the bridge, Mmm? Bygones be bygones?'

He picked up the box and stood up.

'Sure, Dad,' the little Bells chorussed primly, 'No hard feelings at all.'

'There'd better not be,' Big Bob replied, 'or heads will roll.' And he backed out of the kitchen, his eyes never leaving them.

After Big Bob had left, the little Bells continued eating without a word to one another. Then, as though there had been a signal, Angelina stood up and pushed her chair back, and all the others, except Little Bob, did the same. But before they could leave, Bryony sprang up, side-stepped towards the toaster, deftly grabbed what was behind it, and as the procession moved towards the kitchen door she pushed past and stood, hands on hips and legs apart, barring their exit.

'What's this?' whined Melissa.

'We are in no mood for childish games, Bryony,' said Melody.

'We're in a hurry, Bryony,' said Angelina, giving her a push. 'We've a rehearsal to go to...'

'We can't hang around all day playing,' Emmy-Lou put in, pulling at Bryony's right knee. 'Not like some.'

But Bryony stood her ground. She held the piece of paper up to the wall and, very slowly and deliberately, stuck its four corners down with the Blu-Tak. The little Bells each gave a gasp as they surveyed it.

What on earth ...?'

'Over my dead body!'

'Blimey!'

'"Bell Family Duty Rota – Phase 1 – Mornings" ... You have to be joking!'

'No,' said Bryony simply. 'I have never been more serious in my life.'

'But– but–' Angelina began.

'But *you* do breakfast!' whined Melissa, looking more like a Cairn terrier with distemper than ever before.

'Correction,' said Bryony, holding up one finger, which was a technique borrowed from Mrs Ogilvie. 'I *did* breakfast. I've always done breakfast because you always have to do your singing practice. But something's come up. I have demands on my time too. So, until further notice, we're all going to chip in.'

The little Bells opened their mouths to protest, took one look at Bryony's finger, and closed them again. Little Bob started to wail.

'Cut that out!' Bryony shouted, glaring at him and then at her sisters, as though they might start wailing too. She picked up Big Bob's cereal spoon, wiped it on her nightie, and pointed at the Duty Rota. 'I want you all to listen very carefully – I will say this only once.' She tapped the chart.

'You will see that this Duty Rota contains all the morning tasks,' she explained. 'Each task has a code name and a specific colour. For example, "Set table" is denoted by the pink letters "S.T."

'"Wash dishes", similarly, is denoted by the green letters "W.D", and so on. In time, it is to be hoped, we will become so familiar with the system we will no longer need letters.

'I may even introduce a series of coloured badges. '

There were four sharp intakes of breath and

one small gurgle. The little Bells looked at one another, aghast.

'Now – down this side,' Bryony went on, running the spoon down the left column, 'we have the days of the week, and across the top are our names. You will see that I have, for the moment, omitted Little Bob on grounds of age.' She flashed Little Bob a warning glance. 'But as soon as he's potty-trained, he mucks in with the rest of us! Any questions?'

The atmosphere was electric. For a few sizzling seconds no one said anything, and then everyone spoke at once.

'You mean to say you're expecting us to make breakfast and clear up?'

'Where's everything kept?'

'Wash dishes? What about our nails?

'How are we going to fit in our morning practice?'

Bryony held up her finger again.

'The answers to your questions,' she announced firmly, 'in the order of asking, are:

1. Yes, and about time too

2. You'll learn;

3. Wear rubber gloves;

and 4. Get up half an hour earlier like I have to!

'Do I make myself clear?'

Everyone looked at their feet, but no one asked anything else. Bryony replaced the spoon on the table, then turned to consult the Duty Rota. 'Right, then' she said thoughtfully, 'today's Saturday ...' She traced her finger along the top of the chart till she came to the turquoise letters 'S.M.T.', then slid it up to the 'Names' row.

'...So it's Emmy-Lou to set Mum's tray,' she announced, 'Melody to wash dishes, Angelina to dry, and Melissa to put away. OK – break a leg!'

And, in a flurry of pink nylon, Bryony spun round and marched out. She walked slowly up the stairs listening to the chaos in the kitchen, then went into her bedroom, closed the door, and skipped round and round her bed.

'I did it! I did it! I did it!' she chanted. Then she got dressed, did her hair up in her extra-special pink and red rosebud elastics, and thundered back down. As she reached the kitchen she heard a crash and the sound of water hitting the floor from a great height. She considered ignoring it all and making her escape, then realised the greyish-white rollerskates were still on the flowerpots in the shed so, gritting her teeth, she opened the kitchen door again.

A scene of utter mayhem greeted her. The only person who was not in enormous distress was Little Bob, who was rocking to and fro in his high chair, gurgling and cooing with delight and singing *Bob the Builder* more raucously than usual.

Melody, wearing a large pair of pink rubber gloves on the wrong hands, was surveying with horror the shattered remains of the milk-jug. Angelina, her head down and knocked almost senseless by her braids, was dabbing at the kitchen floor – which was awash with soapy water – with the tip of a tartan oven glove. Melissa, holding three teaspoons and peering shortsightedly through her fringe, had just closed the microwave having realised it was not a cutlery cupboard after all, and was standing staring at the row of cereal bowls as though they had just beamed down from Planet Zargon. And Emmy-Lou, who appeared to have lost the will to live, was sitting on the kitchen table surrounded by broken eggshells, crying her eyes out.

As Bryony tried to slink out past them, they all glared accusingly at her.

'And where might you be going?' Angelina asked.

Bryony gave her the loftiest look she could muster.

'If it's any of your business,' she said haughtily, 'I have an important casting meeting.'

She threw open the kitchen door, made her exit, then turned and poked her head back in.

'Just a little production I'm starring in,' she said, casually. 'Toodle-oo!'

Eight

Abid's house was a well-appointed villa on the better side of town. Bryony looked with approval at the stone lions that guarded the front door and the neat tubs of red and white geraniums set out in rows on the sparkling pink gravel as she waited for the doorbell to be answered.

When Mrs Ashraf opened the door she sent out a fragrant cloud of sandalwood. Bryony stood, blinking in disbelief. How could big, shambling Abid have such a small, elegant mother? She had the neatest, shiniest hair Bryony had ever seen, coiled stylishly round her head. She had three gold earrings in each ear, set with rubies and sapphires, one glistening gold ball in the side of her nose, and a golden jewel-encrusted necklace. Her lips were deepest red and her eyes deepest brown. She looked more like a film star than anyone Bryony had ever seen.

'I'm Bryony,' she managed to tell her. 'Abid's friend.'

'Oh yes – Bryony!' When Mrs Ashraf smiled, she looked even more exquisitely beautiful than before. 'Abid's always talking about you. Do come in, it is so nice to meet you at last!'

Bryony followed Mrs Ashraf into the hall. The floor was white marble like the lions and when she paused to take off her rollerskates Mrs Ashraf said, 'Oh don't worry about that, dear! Just freewheel through to the living room,' and she led the way.

Rollerskating on white marble was the most delicious experience Bryony had ever had. It was the equivalent – in skating terms – of wearing silk. There was no resistance – not like the pavement, and certainly not like shagpile. Surreptitiously, she did a little spin. Cosmic!

'Abid's not up yet,' Mrs Ashraf said, then went back out to the hall and roared, 'Get out of your pit, you lazy article!' in an unexpectedly earsplitting voice.

And it was as Mrs Ashraf wafted out that Bryony's heart really turned over. Because the other utterly mind-blowing thing about Mrs Ashraf was what she was wearing. It was, thought Bryony, OUT OF THIS WORLD.

'It's like waking the dead, Bryony,' Mrs Ashraf sighed, coming back in. 'What can I get you, dear? Milk? Coke? A chocolate biscuit?'

But Bryony could only nod. Never in her life had she seen material like the material of Mrs Ashraf's salwar kameez. One minute it looked blue, the next it looked green. It was like some wonderful liquid, or the wing of an exotic bird, its colours glowing and flowing into one another as if by magic.

But that wasn't all. The top part was long and slinky, and its front glittered with gold embroidery and sequins and tiny mirrors. Then, because there were two big slits in its sides, you could see the trousers below had gold pleated inserts so that, when Mrs Ashraf moved, they whirled out like gilded ballet skirts.

'I'll have a glass of Coke, please,' Bryony managed to say, and then: 'I just adore your salwar kameez.'

Mrs Ashraf smiled and wrinkled her nose. 'Oh, this old thing!' she laughed. 'But this is terribly old-fashioned, sweetie. Very retro! You should see the suits I've just stitched for my daughters in London.'

'May I?' asked Bryony eagerly.

'Of course – they're in the kitchen. Come on!'

* * *

Bryony had never imagined such dresses as the ones that hung all around Abid's kichen could exist. There was a white one, studded with tiny pearls, with whorls of silver beads the size of pinheads; there was a black one with even wider inserts than Mrs Ashraf's, that were embroidered with golden flowers and birds and set with thousands of bright black glass beads; and – best of all – there was a pink one with just a hint of purply-lilac shooting through it, covered with layers of paler pink net so it looked as though it had been frosted over, or lightly dusted with icing sugar.

'Oh, Mrs Ashraf!' Bryony breathed. 'These are died-and-gone-to-heaven dresses!' And she held the pink one gently against her cheek and sighed in utter rapture.

Mrs Ashraf poured out some Coke, set three chocolate biscuits and four pieces of pistachio burfee on a plate, and motioned to Bryony to sit down. As she did, a very dishevelled Abid appeared and slumped down at the table opposite. Beside his mother, he looked huger and untidier than ever.

'Hi, Abid!' Bryony said brightly.

'Oh, hi, Bryony,' Abid replied, giving a little cough. 'Have you come about the you-know-what?' He flashed Bryony a warning look and glanced at his mother.

'Eh ... yes ... The 'homework problem', Abid. Thought maybe we could discuss it while we're both fresh.'

Abid yawned, coughed again, and nodded.

'I must leave you both,' Mrs Ashraf said, gathering up the dresses. She rested her chin on Abid's head as she passed, and beamed across the table at Bryony. 'We're terribly grateful to you, Bryony, you know, for sticking up for Abid.

'He's such a baby sometimes. It's with him being the only boy, you know – spoilt rotten.'

She nuzzled into Abid's neck and Abid smiled long-sufferingly.

'Do you know, Bryony,' Mrs Ashraf went on, 'that it took Abid till he was three to get out of nappies? He just hated his little potty, didn't you, Abid?'

'Mum!' Abid hissed, trying to shake himself free. 'Bryony doesn't want to know the details of my toilet-training.'

'Anyway, Bryony,' Mrs Ashraf continued, 'we know you're a great support to him.' She moved round the table till she was beside Bryony. The bundle of dresses glittered and glistened and winked.

'Just supposing you were to have the dress of your dreams, Bryony,' she said softly, 'what would it be like?'

Bryony hardly hesitated. 'It would be pink,' she said decisively, 'and it would have little mirrors round the yoke like yours, and gold embroidery like yours. And the trouser legs would have huge pleated bits in exactly the same colour as yours.'

'Kingfisher blue inserts in a pink salwar kameez?' Mrs Ashraf said doubtfully. 'Really?'

'Really,' said Bryony. 'And a top that's got pleats too so when you spin round it spreads out ... That'd be hard though, wouldn't it?'

'Mmm' said Mrs Ashraf. 'Maybe.'

Bryony bit into her third piece of pistachio burfee and thought rather sadly about Angelina's blue sailor dress.

'Though, actually,' Mrs Ashraf was saying, 'I like a challenge. Adds spice to life!'

Bryony chewed thoughtfully.

Liked a challenge, did she?

She raised her eyebrows at Abid. Another little gem of an idea had just begun to sparkle. She turned to Mrs Ashraf.

'Do you think we could use the hall for our homework meeting, please?' she asked her.

'Certainly, dear,' Mrs Ashraf said. 'But do take cushions. That cold marble's very bad for the back passage, as Abid will testify...'

'Mum' Abid protested, getting up to hold the door open for her, then closing it with relief.

'Your mum's incredible,' Bryony said, as he sat back down. 'Those dresses! Give her a bit of media exposure, Abid, and there's no knowing where she could end up.'

Abid gulped some Coke and looked doubtfully at Bryony.

'Do you think so, Bryony?' he said. Then he brightened up a little. 'She'd be in her element in the world of showbiz,' he sighed. 'Loves the limelight, does Mum. That's why she pushes me to go on the stage, you know. Wants me to fulfill her dreams of stardom.

'Maybe if she'd her own stage career she'd lay off me.' Then he gave himself a little shake. 'Ain't going to happen though, is it,' he said sadly. 'Now – what about this swan thing, Bryony? Had any more breathtakingly-brilliant, scintillatingly-surefire gems of ideas?'

Bryony was just about to tell Abid the sad news of the loss of the Viper 3000s when Big Bob's words flashed into her head. She stood up and led the way to the kitchen door and out into the wonderful silky-smooth rink that was Abid's hall.

'Come on, Abid,' she called. 'Hope you're in good voice this morning, 'cause I need you to sing for me.'

'Sing for you?' Abid cleared his throat nervously.

'You betcha!' smiled Bryony. 'Sing, watch, and be amazed – be very amazed!'

Then she skated out into the middle of the hall and spun so fast on its icy surface that Abid's jaw dropped right down to his knees.

Nine

Monday morning dawned bright and clear, and as soon as Bryony opened her eyes she knew that this was the perfect day to put her plan into action. The sweet smell of success hung in the air.

Her rollerskates dangled expectantly over the bedside lamp. The night before, Big Bob had helped her give them six more applications of shoe whitener and, provided you narrowed your eyes, they looked really quite convincing. She bounced out of bed and eased them into her schoolbag, supporting them carefully between *Physics is Fun* and *Spelling Without Tears*.

As she brushed her hair and selected a pair of white rosebud hair ties, she noted with satisfaction that the house was filled with the sounds of breakfast preparation, and as she sauntered down to take her place at the table she met Angelina carrying Clarissa's tray up to her. Bryony gave her sister an encouraging nod, then stopped, hooked her by the elbow, and held up a finger.

'What?' said Angelina crossly. Her face was very red and some of her braids had unravelled in the effort of S.M.T.

'I believe we have overlooked the rose, have we not?' Bryony pointed out.

'Oh no!' sighed Angelina, turning back to the kitchen.

'Don't worry,' Bryony called after her encouragingly. 'You'll soon get the hang of it!' And she went to inspect the breakfast table.

'Very nice,' she complimented Melissa, who was munching a large slice of toast.

The toast was spread thickly with a lumpy brown substance studded with pink and orange sugary shapes, and Melissa had a rather odd expression on her face as she ate.

'... though you'll find we don't actually need mango chutney or crystallised fruits at breakfast,' Bryony observed.

Melissa paused mid-bite, peered through her fringe at the toast, then continued to eat in bemused silence.

'So when is this performance you're starring in, Bryony?' Melody asked through a mouthful of cereal. 'Some little school thing, is it?'

Bryony reached for the crystal flower-vase and poured milk from it into her tea. 'It may be a "little school thing", Melody,' she told her, 'but you mark my words – it's going to be a groundbreaking "little school thing".'

'And you're the star?' Emmy-Lou asked, gazing at Bryony with eyes like big blue plates. She turned to Melody. 'But Bryony can't sing...' she said quizzically. 'Can't be a star if you can't sing, sure you can't?'

Bryony swallowed a few mouthfuls of cereal and rose from the table just as Big Bob came in with Little Bob at his heels.

'All right if I leave the washing-up this morning, Dad?' she asked. Melissa and Melody and Emmy-Lou's mouths opened in unison, but Big Bob winked and nodded.

'No problem, Bryony,' he said. 'Special dispensation this week – your dad'll do your duties for you. Least he can do!'

And, to a chorus of 'That's not f-a-i-r', Bryony marched haughtily out.

* * *

At the gates of Peachtree Primary, Abid was waiting nervously.

'All set, Abid?' Bryony said, giving his big arm a gentle punch, and Abid wheezed and nodded in reply. He appeared to have lost the power of speech. 'Come on then,' Bryony went on, pulling him by the sleeve, 'to the staffroom, before it fills up. You know what they say, – "The early bird catches the worm"!'

The 'worm', in the shape of Mrs Quigg, was the only teacher in place at that time of the morning, and when Bryony knocked she called 'You may enter!' and glared over her little half-moon spectacles at her.

'Might Abid and I have a quick word, Mrs Quigg?' Bryony said, as calmly as she could.

'If it's about the 'Swan' part, Bryony,' Mrs Quigg said wearily, picking up a large mug of coffee and taking several slugs, 'I shall be extremely annoyed.'

Bryony paused. You had to hand it to her, she thought – Mrs Quigg was one sharp lady.

'Well...' she began. 'It is, and it isn't...'

At this, Mrs Quigg rolled her eyes heavenward. For a moment, Bryony thought she was going to shout at her. But instead she did something far, far worse.

'You, Bryony Bell,' she said tremulously, 'do not understand the artistic soul. You are simply unable to appreciate the months of creative work that went in to writing *The Ugly Duckling*.' She withdrew a crumpled handkerchief from her sleeve and dabbed her nose and eyes. 'The pain,' she continued, 'the heartache, the burning of the midnight oil ...

'And you ...' Mrs Quigg struggled to her feet and pointed a trembling finger at Bryony, '... you would ruin it! You would trample the fruits of my labour under your feet! You would burst my bubbles, bring my dreams tumbling down...'

Abid, who had crept into the staffroom behind Bryony, took a few steps towards Mrs Quigg.

'You wrote the play, Mrs Quigg?' he said, in tones of wonder. Mrs Quigg blew her nose and nodded.

'And the songs?' Bryony gasped.

Mrs Quigg nodded again.

'Wow!' exclaimed Abid.

'Awesome!' breathed Bryony.

'And I don't mind telling you both,' Mrs Quigg went on, a little more calmly, 'that I consider *The Swan Song* to be my *tour de force*.'

Bryony and Abid exchanged puzzled looks.

'My crowning achievement,' Mrs Quigg explained. 'The minute I found that swan costume in the Oxfam shop, I was inspired. It spoke to me.'

She sighed, slumped back down on her chair, and took a few more gulps of coffee.

'To see Abid wearing it, and singing so divinely,' she went on, 'means more to me than words can say...'

There was a long and awkward silence, then Bryony spoke.

'I'm really, really sorry, Mrs Quigg,' she said. 'I never wanted to ruin the play. I wanted to make it better. It's a brilliant play, and I think it's just wicked that you wrote it—'

Bryony stopped, mid-sentence, and stared. She could hardly believe her eyes. Abid, without a hint of a wheeze or a cough, was stepping boldly right up to the music teacher and putting a large hand on her shoulder.

'We're with you all the way, Mrs Quigg,' he said, looking at her steadily. 'Why don't you come to the hall with us? Just keep an open mind – please?'

They both looked imploringly at Mrs Quigg.

'We've been burning the midnight oil too,' Bryony said, coming to stand opposite Abid. They each slipped a hand under the teacher's arms and eased her up.

'We've got artistic souls too, Bryony and me,' Abid added unexpectedly, steering Mrs Quigg gently in the direction of the door.

Much to their surprise and relief, Mrs Quigg allowed herself to be led out of the staffroom and along the corridor to the hall, where Bryony and Abid sat her down at the piano.

'Give us three minutes to get ready, Mrs Quigg,' whispered Bryony. 'Then play the introduction to the Swan Song.'

Like someone in a hypnotic trance Mrs Quigg sat, hands hovering above the piano keys, gazing up at the empty stage.

'We've got a bit of a *tour de force* too,' explained Abid, lifting the piano lid and setting *The Ugly Duckling* music in position.

'So prepare to be blown away.'

Ten

On the night of *The Ugly Duckling* show, the hall of Peachtree Primary was filled to maximum capacity. Mrs Quigg, nicely done up in a high-collared white blouse and with her curls an interesting shade of blue, played a medley of *Ugly Duckling* songs to get everyone in the mood as they settled into their seats.

In the front row sat Big Bob, Angelina, Melody, Melissa, Emmy-Lou, and Clarissa with Little Bob on her lap. Mrs Ashraf, looking more elegant than ever in a lavender and gold salwar kameez, was sandwiched between Clarissa and Dr Ashraf, both of whom took up rather more than one seat. Everyone was full of excited anticipation, although the little Bell girls were careful not to appear too keen. Their icy feelings had all but defrosted, but there was still a bit of a nip in the air.

From time to time, Big Bob would dab the perspiration off his brow and dart worried glances at his family. Something was weighing heavily on his mind. After tea that evening he had taken Bryony to one side and, without a word, had led her to the potting shed. Bryony, bewildered, had watched the door swing slowly open and when she saw what was sitting inside she had been quite unable to speak.

'I couldn't do it, Bryony,' Big Bob had said at last. 'I know it was wrong of me, but the longer I stood in the queue at the Post Office the more I thought I just couldn't hand them over. Tonight's your big night, and I'd never forgive myself if you didn't have your Vipers ...

'I've the wrapping all ready, lass, and as soon as the show's over they go straight back in the box and away. There's still two days' approval, and one performance won't harm them.'

Bryony had not known what to say. The Viper 3000s, sitting on top of their box, looked even whiter and ligher and shinier than she remembered – and she was going to wear them, one last time, for *The Swan Song*! It was too much to take in.

'Now don't you worry, Bryony,' Big Bob had told her as he handed her the Vipers. 'You just do your very best – and if there's any trouble, your Dad'll take the flack.'

'OK, Dad,' Bryony had whispered at last, cradling the skates. 'I'll give it my all.'

* * *

The blue velvet stage curtains twitched open to reveal a very small boy wearing a shiny grey suit and red bow tie. Jeremy, who had fallen off the log so often that his mother had filed an official complaint, had had his frog suit taken from him and been given the important job of Master of Ceremonies and Narrator.

'Good evening, ladies, gentlemen and children,' he announced carefully, 'and welcome to our show. It's called *The Ugly Duckling* and ...' He looked down desperately.

'We hope you ...' came Mrs Quigg's stage-whisper.

'We hope you will enjoy it,' Jeremy finished with a sigh of relief. Then he side-stepped off with his right arm outstretched, and as he did the curtains swished open to reveal the first scene where the farmyard animals were telling each other about the strange egg that was about to crack.

Next came the part by the lake and the frogs' log. Mrs Quigg played the opening bars of the Frogs' Chorus with gusto, and they all began to sing. And when Bryony made her entrance as the Ugly Duckling and the frogs bounced up and down and laughed at her, there was no risk of anyone falling off the log, for Abid had been persuaded to don

Jeremy's green Lycra and sit at the end, acting as balast.

This part, as hoped, brought the house down, and when it was over the audience applauded with vigour. There were a number of other songs as the Ugly Duckling was made to feel more and more miserable, and at last it was time for the winter scene. The lights dimmed and a big white sheet, cunningly concealed behind the log, was carefully unrolled and draped over everything to create the impression of snow. Two little girls dressed as snowflakes tiptoed on and scattered white glitter, and above it all Jeremy's voice told how the Ugly Duckling had hidden itself away, unable to bear the constant humiliation. It was all very poignant.

'But when the spring came, and the snow melted ...' Jeremy went on, pausing to let the snowflakes skip back in and remove the sheet, '... something very strange, and very wonderful, happened ...'

One by one all the frogs except Abid hopped back onstage and repositioned themselves on the log. Then the lights came on, bathing everyone in a beautiful rosy light. Mrs Quigg glanced up to make sure the stage was set, then played the rippling introduction to *The Swan Song*.

And then, like a smoothly shimmering dream, Bryony Bell made her entrance.

Never, as Clarissa said afterwards, was an entrance so entrancing! The whole hall seemed to take a big breath and hold it as the swan glided in balanced on one leg with the other held out behind her, straight as a die. The huge swan costume had been well and truly redesigned by Abid's mother who, happily accepting the challenge, had removed its feathers and had attached them to a sparkling-white bodice onto which she had sewn a silver-sequined swan. The sleeves were long and tight-fitting and culminated in white feathery cuffs that wafted delicately about as Bryony sped across the stage; and in her hair there nestled a feathery silver-and-white tiara, which glistened under the lights.

More gracefully and silently than ever a swan swam, Bryony floated round the stage and past the frog log, where she stopped, turned on one foot, and rotated faster and faster with her head flung back.

Then, skating backwards to the edge of the stage so fast that everyone in the front row gasped and lifted their feet onto their chairs, she went into a spin dangerously near Mrs Quigg's head, to finish with both arms in the air, as still as a statue. Practising the routine in Abid's marble hall with her old skates had been wonderful – but being on a wooden stage with the Vipers was quite out of this world. There was no resistance at all. It was like skating on air.

For a moment Bryony paused and surveyed her audience, then pushed off again to centre stage where she sank down on the blue cloth lake and inclined her head to one side, looking into the wings. Automatically everyone in the audience followed her gaze, and then the first strains of Abid's song rang out more purely and clearly and confidently than ever before.

I look at my reflection, Abid sang,
And it looks back at me
And what I see there in the lake
Is what I want to see

Mrs Quigg played a few little tinkly bars during which Bryony took a last lingering look at herself in the blue cloth, unfolded her legs, and stood up. As the next verse was sung she circled the log, giving each frog in turn a little pat. At rehearsal, Bryony had argued the case for banging all their heads together, but Mrs Quigg had warned her she had to 'chastise them with decorum' for fear of more complaints from parents.

I had such dowdy feathers, Abid's voice rang out,
You laughed and laughed at me
But now I'm very beau-ti-ful
As you can plainly see...

During the next tinkly bit, Bryony skated round to face the audience. As Abid sang the last verse, she looked all along the front row and smiled at each member of her family in turn, noting happily that every one of them smiled back at her in utter admiration.

And so here is my message, Abid trilled,
Don't ever try to hide
Just hold your head up, show the world
The 'swan' you've got inside!

Bryony turned to the logful of frogs and they all got up, gripped her round the knees, and hoisted her high above their heads. All around them, the stage began to fill as farmyard ducks and goats and geese and chickens filed in, and when the whole cast was on stage everyone sang the last verse again, very slowly and loudly. As they did they joined hands to form an arch through which Abid, his frog mask under his arm, made his entrance and modestly bowed.

For a moment everyone in the hall was still as Mrs Quigg's last note hung in the air, and then the whole hall exploded into tumultuous applause. People stood up and waved their programmes about, children stamped their feet, and everyone whooped and clapped and cried 'Encore!' And when, just above the racket, Bryony heard Emmy-Lou say, 'That's my big sister, so it is!', she thought her chest would burst with pride.

The frogs let Bryony down and she curtseyed gracefully, holding the white feathers carefully between the tips of her fingers. Then both Bryony and Abid linked arms and pointed to Mrs Quigg, who stood, faced the audience, and gave a stiff little bow.

Tears of emotion made little pale furrows in Clarissa's foundation cream. Mrs Ashraf dabbed her immaculate cheeks with a moist wipe and whispered 'That's my boy' over and over again. And at each end of the front row the proud fathers blew their noses into their big handkerchiefs, and glowed and glowed with pride.

* * *

Over the hubbub, Jeremy had announced that tea and biscuits would be served in the staffroom, and when Abid and Bryony finally escaped Mrs Quigg's embraces and found their way there, Bryony had her heart in her mouth. The play, she knew, had been a tour de force if ever there was one, but what would Mum and the little 'uns say about the Vipers?

'How was it for you, Abid?' she asked as they fought their way through the audience, every one of whom wanted to congratulate them. To her relief, Abid beamed.

'It was cool, Bryony,' he said. 'I do love

singing, you know. Just not having people watch me sing.' He paused to sign his name on the back of a small boy's hand. 'Maybe,' he said thoughtfully, 'I could perform on the radio...'

The Bells and the Ashrafs were standing together in a huddle by the window. When she saw Bryony Clarissa ran towards her, big arms outstretched.

'Oh Bryony, love,' she said, giving Bryony an almighty kiss on the cheek, then wiping off the lipstick mark, 'you were splendid! Wasn't she?' She glanced over at the little 'uns, who all nodded vehemently.

'The best,' said Melody.

'Professional to the last,' said Angelina, sincerely.

'Unbelievable,' sighed Melissa.

And Emmy-Lou buried her face in the white feathers of Bryony's skirt, looked up at her, and said, 'I wish you could skate with *The Singing Bells*, Bryony!'

'Yeee-hah!' Big Bob called, slapping his thigh. 'Champion idea, Emmy-Lou.' He looked over at Clarissa. 'What d'you think, Clarissa? *The Singing, Skating Bells*? Something to think about for the future?'

Clarissa looked thoughtful. Then she nodded. 'Could have legs,' she said.

'Course,' continued Big Bob,' she'd have to

keep the Viper 3000s. Couldn't have her on TV with tatty old skates ...'

Throughout all this, Bryony said nothing. She was so deliriously happy, it felt as though her brain had gone into overdrive.

And, as if all this wasn't enough, Mrs Ashraf was coming towards her with a shiny red parcel done up with a gold ribbon.

'This is to thank you, Bryony, for everything you've done for Abid,' she said, laying it in Bryony's arms. 'And to congratulate you on your wonderful performance.

'I hope it's what you wanted.'

Bryony undid the wrapping and held the contents up.

It was the outfit of her dreams – a bright pink salwar kameez with little mirrors at the yoke, gold embroidery, and pleated kingfisher-blue inserts in the trousers. The top was pleated too, and you could just imagine how it would spread out when you spun. It was exactly, precisely, what Bryony had imagined.

'Oh thank you, Mrs Ashraf,' she managed to say.

'You'll be the belle of the ball tonight Bryony,' Big Bob whispered.

'It's the most beautiful thing I ever saw,' breathed Angelina.

'Oh my goodness,' said Clarissa, holding one

of the shiny pink sleeves out and talking very quickly, 'isn't this exactly the sort of thing that'd get us noticed on TV? Imagine the *Devoted Sisters* song and dance! Pure theatre, it would be, in these!'

The little Bells all nodded and jumped up and down.

'You couldn't run up another five before next week, Mrs Ashraf – could you?' Clarissa asked. 'Oh no – of course you couldn't.'

Mrs Ashraf looked questioningly from Abid to Dr Ashraf. Dr Ashraf beamed and spoke for the first time that evening.

'I think she could,' he told Clarissa. 'Shabana can do anything if she turns her mind to it!'

Mrs Ashraf took the dress from Bryony and held it against Clarissa. She looked her up and down, one eye closed.

'I'd advise a sari for you, dear,' she said at last. 'Same materials, same embroidery, but the cut is so much more flattering to the fuller figure.' Then she beamed at Clarissa and Big Bob. 'Would I get a mention in the credits, do you think?'

'I'm sure it could be arranged,' Big Bob said confidently. 'How about 'Costumes by Shabana Ashraf, Designer to the Stars'?'

'Consider it done,' said Abid's mother, without a moment's hesitation. She reached inside her handbag for a measuring tape and a notepad and pencil, which she handed to Abid. 'It'll be my gateway to a stage career,' she said excitedly, running the tape up and down each little Bell in turn.

'So we'll think of it as a publicity exercise,' she went on. 'And I'll just charge you for the material.'

The Bells looked at Mrs Ashraf. They gazed, unbelieving, at one another.

'So...' Clarissa said slowly, 'It wouldn't cost the Earth?'

'Hardly anything at all, dear,' Mrs Ashraf said. 'Are you getting this down, Abid?'

Abid went on scribbling into the notepad. Every single Bell eye fell on Bryony's feet and the Viper 3000s.

'You thinking what I'm thinking?' Big Bob said to Clarissa.

Clarissa smiled a huge red smile.

'I am,' she said. ' And I'm thinking the same. Those skates ain't going anywhere but our Bryony's feet!'

Speechless, Bryony hugged her salwar kameez. Its pinkness made her face glow, and tiny rainbows of light reflected onto her chin from its mirrors. Happiness spread from her silver tiara to the tips of her Viper-clad toes. She put her arm round Big Bob's shoulders and gave him a squeeze.

'You said I'd get the Vipers one day, or your name's not Bob Bell,' she said.

'Sure did, princess,' Big Bob said, beaming admiringly up at her.

'And I'll tell you another thing, Bryony,' he added softly. 'You'll always be top of my bill!'

About the Author

Franzeska G Ewart was born in Stranraer – a small town by the sea in Galloway. She spent her childhood in the countryside and down on the seashore and she still likes to go there and to wander about in the woods and along riverbanks.

She then went on to study Zoology at Glasgow University, before deciding that she wanted to teach and going on to study for her Primary Teaching Certificate.

Franzeska lives in Glasgow – full-time with her cat Lily, and part-time with her partner Adam. She loves gardening, painting, writing, music, frogs and cats – though probably in reverse order.

For many years Franzeska used shadow theatre to help people express themselves. These days, she still works part-time in Glendale Primary School teaching English as an Additional Language. The children and staff there often appear in her books!

Franzeska has had over a dozen books for children published. These include *Speak Up Spike*, *Shadowflight* and *The Pen-pal from Outer Space* which were all named *Guardian* Book of the Week.

About Bryony Bell Tops the Bill:

My inspiration for Bryony was a girl who came to one of my author talks. She had very bubbly blonde hair in two bunches, held in place with terrribly fancy flowers, and she was really COOL. I just liked her style, and I thought she'd be really assertive and capable and extrovert but would also love frills and flounces and sparkles. Just like Bryony!

Another fantastic Black Cat ...

JAN MARK
Eyes wide open

Six brilliantly-crafted short stories from
a master of the form.

Discover how the tooth fairy turned one
boy into a millionaire; how a reflection
in a department store mirror unlocked
a family's dark secret, and find out
how a misunderstood message
transforms two boys' journey on the
London Underground into a
comedy-adventure.

These stories deserve, and will reward, a wide readership.
Lindsey Fraser *The Guardian*

Another fantastic Black Cat ...

SUE PURKISS
Changing Brooms

Jess longs to train to become a
proper witch, but her family can't
afford the tuition fees, and so she's
stuck being an apprentice to
Agnes Moonthistle, whose services
as a witch aren't at all in demand –
because she's not very good.
However, when the TV programme,
Changing Brooms, offers the chance
to use magic to win ten thousand
pounds, Jess may have found
her escape route ...

Black Cats – collect them all!